The '.

The road at 3:00 AM disappeared into the blackness. At top speed the islands of light blurred by. One by one in a rhythmic flashing, leading to more darkness. The radio program did its best to keep the heavy nighttime silence away.

Bethany Ultrix felt it though, she felt the silence of a late-night drive. The kind of silence that is a fresh field for the rotten fruits of frustration. There had been a fight, the first one in a long time and the wounds needed a deeper darkness. Bethany switched the radio program off and let the weight of the night press down.

The fight was a flame lick, a smoldering dissatisfaction that finally burnt its way out. Once the fire was seen, they both grabbed their knives and sunk them into each other. After the figurative blood bath, after the smell started to seep in. A rift began forming, a wedge made of fresh burns and quick knives. It all happened so fast. There was little thinking, just the quick reactions of self-preservation.

Now the fight was over, the wounds weeping out their unforgettable words. When the wedge got too big, when the room was full of smoke and blood, it became time to drive. Bethany loved driving, even with all the vehicular applications, there is nothing quite like holding the wheel yourself.

More than once she felt the darkness sink its teeth into her and the lure of driving off into oblivion made its case. There is time enough for that later she thought, the pain was still fresh. The words could not be unspoken, they couldn't be bottled back up and swallowed.

They were free now, bitter shadows that jumped from lamppost to lamppost, following Bethany's vehicle.

She was driving to her friend's house, an old friend that kept their door open. She drove through the night; each hour fermented the fight into a sour mash. By the early and dark morning, the words had decayed into streams of tears. She was exhausted, unable to think, unwilling to let the shadow go. Bethany needed sleep, her brain was sounding the alarm for unconsciousness.

Her friend's house was hidden on the far side of a national forest. It was tucked neatly at the end of a gravel road. It was shrouded by old Madronas, twisted trees with red and orange arms. They waved with shadows as the headlights washed over them. Bethany drove up sharp switchbacks until she reached her friend's house.

Bethany Ultrix walked into the dark duplex and collapsed on the couch, she pulled a blanket up over her head and fell fast into the darkness. Her sleep was monolithic, an unchanging void for a few short moments. The sun was high in the sky before any thoughts filled her head. The wounds in her heart still hurt but they seemed far away in the early moments of the warm afternoon.

She made some coffee, splashed some water on her face and sat back on the couch with a large ceramic mug. Her device glowed from across the room with messages, she ignored them. She knew what they said, she knew what waited for her back at home, she wanted none of it. She wanted nothing at all, she wanted to sip on her coffee forever, she wanted to curl back up into the darkness and go back to sleep.

She didn't want to rejoin the land of the living again, the wedge had grown over the evening, it had stretched itself over the great space between the fight and the daylight outside. She could feel the rift. She could feel the rift like a vise on her head, she could feel the shadows swirling inside. Tears fell into her coffee as the previous evening played out repetitively until the coffee was cold.

After the cold coffee was finished, she made some more. The bitter coffee grounds were no match for the bright heartache. The second evening stretched out into a nervous caffeine coma. Anxious and energized, her imagination spun out into a paralyzing pit of doubt. What happens next? The hurt is too much to get past, the words can not be unspoken, the wounds can't be forgotten.

Bethany tried to sleep, she tried to push the ideas away. She tiptoed around unconsciousness, each time she got close the memory of the fight would take another stab. By the morning she was even more exhausted, and her heart had sunk further. Unable to pull out of the nosedive into oblivion, Bethany found herself shuffling down into the basement of the dark duplex.

The cement walls made a simple tomb. One wall held a foot locker full of memories, things she hadn't looked at in years. The kind of detritus that builds up over the years; old wounds, tears, love notes, keepsakes, the human trinket system. Bethany's locker was just like anyone else's magic box, it was an ocean of memories, each object was a key to a different time and place.

Bethany wanted to be somewhere else, and she spent the greater part of the third day traveling the topography of her past. When her heart could take no more, when her tears seemed spent, she let out a heavy sigh. She let the weight fall off her heart, she pulled the wedding ring from her hand and dropped it into a black piece of fabric. The fabric was folded neatly and placed with her other dead friends, memories waiting in a tomb to be remembered.

She laid there for a few minutes, saying goodbye to her old friends. Part of her had died, the rift was too large. She put the keepsakes back into the foot locker and cleaned her coffee cups. The crossroads had been traveled, and there was no turning back. She waved goodbye to the Madronas, crawled back out of the forest and began building a new life. She left the door unlocked for next time.

The Witch of November:

Sometimes in the darkest lakes there is a greater blackness that is born. A little seed of shadows that forms a shell of icy water. The seed waits and only grows under very specific circumstances. If these conditions are not met, the seed can drift on the bottom unchanged for years, patient and cruel.

The conditions are quite common for the world of human beings. The seed requires the mournful wailing of loss, whether by ship wreck, heartbreak, suicide or murder. The remnants of those bodies, pieces of those lights that have sunk to the bottom. As they sink to the bottom, they bring with them the tears of those that wept for them.

The seed takes hundreds of bodies, sometimes thousands of mourners pouring their eyes into the waters before the seed grows. Such an event happens once in an age or two. Due to the monolithic force of progress, such seeds have become more common. There are millions more people, millions of mournful, grieving eyes to add their sorrow to the great oceans and lakes of the world.

Some people think the rise of the water is a mechanical consequence, ice caps melting or some such thing. While they are correct, the true cause is the gathering of sorrow. One day such tears may drown the world. There are billions of more suffering human beings, and there will be billions more without a doubt.

The seed grows slowly. The icy shell cracks after decades of a slow and glacial oblivion. Within is a spectral wraith, a white and gray creature that perhaps could be confused with a large jellyfish or giant squid. However, this spectral creature is neither living nor ambivalent.

The phantasm of the deep is born with the icy tears of anguish within its ethereal tendrils, its eyes gleaming out a mournful reflection of the sorrow of the deep waters. From the beginning of its creation, its instinct is clear and its heart black. The white appendages resemble those of a beautiful woman, the wisps surrounding its body appear to be tattered clothes, translucent and rotten. Yet these are only a glamour, an attempt to make sense of such a creature.

For years the ghost may swim on the bottom, searching for a few more bodies drowned in grief, perhaps a lost child or love-sick sailor. Each small meal teases the hunger of the spectre, leaving it more voracious, more eager to rise higher to the surface.

Hunger eventually compels them to the edges of shorelines, harbors and stormy lakes. They follow the cold winds around waiting for shipwrecks. Like vultures waiting for carrion that they encircle patiently, anticipating the inevitable.

One such creature had grown to a great size, due primarily to the winter storms. Her appendages had grown long and lanky, bearing taloned hands of bitter white. She grew very hungry and very eager, eventually she rose to the surface.

It was a lazy November evening, a little fire and friends by a lake. 23 people had gathered in merriment. The Witch of November beached herself while they were cooking marshmallows. Her gigantic mass of wisps and lace rose up nearly 20 feet tall. She floated like an icy fog towards the fire light. Someone shrieked that a woman was coming out of the lake. They stood in terror as the eyes of the Witch looked over them, beaming out decades of sorrow and darkness. The greater blackness from which she came oozed out of her eyes.

There were 3 survivors, the rest had followed the ghost back into the water, overcome with loss. The greater blackness swallowed them whole and the Witch of November sunk down to the deep, temporarily satisfied.

Annually she returns, perhaps to a friendly campsite, a couple walking down the beach, a lonely dock worker or pier fisherman. The brackish waters betray no warning and offer no reason. Her hunger is as senseless as the sorrow that feeds her.

Kingdom of Dust:

There is no wandering into the Kingdom of Dust, there is no ability to roam. You can not walk from one side to the other, nor travel around it. The dimensions of such a place should be perhaps measured in existential terms: It is the place where things decay into obscurity. There is nothing that remains within existence that describes, details or keeps an inventory of these lost things.

The Kingdom of Dust has claimed countless empires, endless cultures, people, nations, basements, attics, oceans of tears, distant stars, and at some point, the Kingdom of Dust will claim existence itself. This is to say; these things are or will be forgotten. They fall back into indistinction and decay into whatever smaller parts they are made of, perhaps used to create new things, perhaps used for nothing at all ever again, useless cogs sitting motionless at the bottom of a cosmic trash pile. Regardless, they cease to be the things that they once were.

Sometimes mere accidents prevent things from falling into its fuzzy territory. Such is the fate of the library of Ashurbanipal. A tongue twister named after a cruel ruler from the 7th Century B.C.E. who collected all sorts of clay tablets, wax scrolls, and papyrus literature of all kinds. This library stood as the brightest flame for its time, a beacon of information and history allowing a type of retrospect that empires build their foundations on.

Of course, such bright beacons of literature are burned, scoured or erased from existence. They plummet quickly into the hazy pages of history, perhaps lasting only a couple generations of living memory. The library was burned sometime around 613 B.C.E., ashes and dirt piled on top to quicken the library's descent into nothingness.

However, the burning of the clay tablets baked them partially, accidentally preserving their contents in a shallow grave. Centuries later, when the library was unearthed, the baked clay tablets had not quite fallen into the Kingdom of Dust. They remained legible, containing the epic of Gilgamesh, a hero story about traveling the torrents of the gods with his savage friend Enkidu. The ancient tale owing its survival to an accidental fire caused by the furnace of revolution.

So, it seems that by luck the tablets survived, by an incidental thermal reaction.

Human beings, with their perception and categorical brains, constant remembering and retelling, have managed to migrate from the Kingdom of Dust. We have found ways to keep the tidal shoreline from rising, we can keep the dust away from the scrolls and the books. We have found more elaborate empires to build, more detailed stories to scribe, allowing, through practical applications; more human beings to exist.

One by one we march from the Kingdom of Dust, our heads blind at birth, and when they close we slip back into the formless boundaries of its territory. It may take a few generations, perhaps we may live in the memories of others for thousands of years. We may forget, in our hubris that empires are mortal, cultures die, people blend into a wider society and their individual qualities disappear. Slowly over the eons all things return to their homeland, they return back into a world of primordial clutter. Like an endless junkyard, guarded by a decrepit Cerberus barking feebly.

If you find some road leading to this cosmic junkyard and look around without recognizing anything. You may find yourself grasping to any definition, any sense of order. You may riffle through the rusted metal and discarded war machines, you may find a deeper understanding through a desperate need for meaning. Some return from the Kingdom of Dust, enthusiastic historians with trinkets from beyond the veil of the lost, some promethean idealist hoping to find some linchpin in the debris of human history.

Those that return are often cloaked in certainty, glowing with an oily and iridescent enlightenment. Like Joseph and his coat of many colors, displaying a dizzying nausea of wonderment. Of course, over time the glamour washes off and the colors run back into the delta of dull meaninglessness. History repeats, the waves of time rise, and all is forgotten again.

This mechanism of forgetting is a small timescale to human beings who rarely experience anything from the larger realms of existences. We may mark our latticed time tables on terrestrial rotations, comets or lunar shadows. We have not experienced star birth, galactic collisions, the churning of nebulas or anything on a time scale of millions of years. We are bound to the graveyard of higher worlds.

This inability extends below as well, to the very small. While we are caught in the torrents of the atomic and microbial, their worlds are often invisible to our categorical minds. We can see their worlds only in concept, microscopes, chemicals and books. Their generations and empires passing so quickly that we often remove them with a sanitary wipe on the kitchen sink. We are typically mindless to the world of the small.

The edge of our awareness seems to be based on time scale and size. When they move we move but without consideration, as if one foot was in the Kingdom of Dust, casually heaped up with all the other feet. When the larger tides of greater blackness move, and a large arrival graces the Kingdom of Dust, we may by way of circumstance be swept away in our entirety. Some gamma ray burst may annihilate every shred of evidence that human beings ever existed. By extension of imagination, an even greater blackness may annihilate the very concept of existence, an idea based solely on the perception of middle minded creatures that writhe in awe at some trinkets they find in the graveyard of the past.

If you find this idea bleak, worry not, for even the loss of all humanity, all existence is simply part of a tide of greater blackness. That everything conceived or inventoried returns to the indistinct realm called the Kingdom of Dust. Perhaps this description may act as a sense of order for those uncomfortable with nothing being anything, with the idea of a cosmic clutter, things without names written on their atoms. That perhaps the torrent of existence isn't anything particular. Perhaps acknowledging existence may be giving it too much credit, and the royal road to the Kingdom of Dust is merely the basement of neglect.

The Move:

Two dozen plastic arms flashed in neon power. A cyclopean tornado of logistical horror whirled through the house. It was time for the big move. Francis had never moved for these reasons before, it was all a new experience. He stood in the doorway as the machines shuffled and packed his belongings, green and red lasers scanned everything. The living room was a buzz with label printers, the bathroom a hiss with scrubbers and the bedroom a muffled flurry of clothes being meticulously sorted.

Francis reflected for a few moments at the eye of the tornado. Before the moving machines existed how had people moved their belongings? They would have to evaluate, categorize, and package all their possessions themselves. Francis reeled in terror; to depend so much on your present mindset, your own organizing skills. If you forgot something or misplaced something, it would be buried in forgotten boxes or tosses into the trash simply because you couldn't remember in the moment.

Francis was going through a breakup, an old relationship. He couldn't imagine the weight of such a task while the loss of his relationship was seeping out of his heart. He tried during those peaceful moments of reflection, but each time his mind recoiled. He went back watching the white and silver moving machines.

Francis trusted the moving machines, they knew his profile completely. All the things that were important and not important, all the tokens and keepsakes of his past. For example: they would not trash a hand-written letter from his mother nor a picture of his first serious girlfriend. They would trash old receipts, useless memories, unlicensed or copyrighted material, anything that didn't fit within his profile.

The white and silver armed machines finished their job within 6 hours. All of Francis's processions were packed and boxed and sent to his new domicile. He trusted them more than he trusted himself, maybe not with everything but he explicitly trusted the system. He walked through his vacated home one last time in somber self-awareness.

He started at the top floor, the bedroom. He remembered the fond times, the warm nights when the moon beamed down her halo of half opened eyes. He sighed, and looked at the empty room, it had been sterilized, emptied and painted already. It was only a shell and all that remained were his memories of the place. Next, he stopped by the kitchen, remembering the delicious dinners and glasses of sultry wine. The candlelight flickered one last time in his heart and then faded into the sterile square the kitchen had become.

Room by room he repeated his invocation of memories and each time the pleasant remnants surfaced and lit up one last time. Then the lights went out, the house was dark and vacant. Francis trusted the system, he had followed the exit instructions precisely. He found that after the exit ritual he could not remember the unpleasant memories, he could not remember her face or her name. He felt a sense of relief, maybe the machines had washed more than his house, it didn't matter anyways. Francis was moving into a new chapter of his life, a new day was waiting for him, all his things would be eager to see him in his new home.

He wondered for a few moments while in transit, he stared out the window and ruminated on his first move. He winced at the idea of being unable to turn away from the unpleasant memories, how did older models function with such a burden? He tried to think about it a little more, but something distracted him on the horizon.

Over the edge of the ocean he saw turbulent black and purple clouds forming, a weather system was moving in. The clouds looked like people in an embrace, something about their motion reminded him of those warm nights in his bedroom, he couldn't see the faces anymore, but he felt something familiar in those clouds. For a brief moment he wished to feel all of it, he wanted to turn off all his fail-safes and get lost in the coming storm, he wanted to get lost in a sky of purple plumes. The haze of the night crept over the ocean and the clouds faded into an opaque blackness before he arrived at his new home.

Francis walked up a stone path to his new home, unlocked the door and a warm wash of euphoria greeted him as everything looked familiar.

New Designation:

Harold Orius #Reflection hour 12:47:

I was 13 when the trucks started moving into town. Fleets of semis carrying construction equipment and shipping containers. I remember the sharp contrast: one week, rolling hillsides and tuna casserole, then the next our town was infested with hardhats.

The invasion descended without any warning, an unstoppable wave of progress. By the next year our town was buried in construction sites and new roads for bigger equipment. I remember my parents wanting to move, but my father was able to get a job at one of the sites and then our family was quiet about the whole thing.

By the time I was getting ready for graduation I knew what the construction was for. They were building a pyramid of shipping containers. Perhaps the size made it hard to determine the monolithic scale or perhaps people were intentionally deceived, either way our skyline was filling up with the steel monument.

The pyramid wasn't recognizable for many years because the base took so long to level and define. Apparently, the size was precisely why our town was chosen, our nowhere town was an ancient flat foot print. The base was 9 miles on each side, making a gigantic collection of shipping containers. They were piled up in heaps like little hills slowly becoming a single mountain.

Harold Orius #Reflection hour 10:27:

There was an explosion today at my dad's site. A storehouse of acetylene made a mortal plume and 12 people were killed. The overseers said it was arson and the company police started to investigate possible leads. My mother has been crying since the news and I feel like I am sinking into the same pit.

We were offered a free burial by the company regardless of the investigation. I don't know if my mother will accept, the burial site is inside of the pyramid within a steel container. They also offered me a job today, I turned 18 a few days ago and I guess they headhunt locals. I am feeling apprehensive about the whole thing and losing my dad makes me want to leave this town.

Harold Orius #Reflection hour 07:29:

I decided to stay, the pay is too good. I looked at other places nearby and unless I want to be a grocery store clerk my options are limited. I started last week and surprisingly enjoy working on such a monolithic project. The hours aren't bad, and I can take care of my mother. She seems to be deep in the pit of mourning.

I found her today when I got home staring out the window over at the slow-motion mountain, she didn't respond even when I called her name. When I touched her arm, she jolted and apologized. She said she was thinking of dad, but I have never seen her so distant.

Today I also learned that they are building underneath the pyramid as well, a system of underground tunnels that lead to normally inaccessible parts of the structure. This pyramid never ceases to surprise me.

Harold Orius #Reflection hour 22:41:

It has been 3 years since my last reflection entry, work has occupied my every hour. The more I work at the pyramid the more amazed I am at the size of the structure. The pyramid is growing upwards faster each week, each layer requires fewer containers and less welding. The cranes seem to be working through the night and the company is handing out overtime bonuses.

There was a bit of an upset in management, apparently the previous company sold the pyramid project to a new techno-religious group called the Church of Loa. Everyone is very hush hush about it, but the Church promised to double my pay if I stayed on after the changeover.

Mother is growing more distant each year, she does nothing but stare at the steel mountain. I found her when I got home with her breakfast plate still on the table. I think I might have to take her to a special care home. The new company offers extended care for relatives of workers. I didn't think I would be a company man, but they are so attentive with their employees.

I have never been someone interested in higher identities. I never liked sports, nationalism or religion. However, this new company and this project has certainly become important to me over the years. I am grateful to be part of such a momentous project.

Horus 5.7 #Reflection hour 02:31:

Last night I was invited to meet one of the Church of Loa clergy. I was getting ready to head to the sleeping rooms and was notified to come to the 2nd layer office.

I was led through a portion of the 3rd layer which seemed like an endless factory line. V-type models were being assembled in different stages. Some of the faces looked human, they looked up at me and smiled, and some were still having their faces constructed. The faceless looked up at me with black and yellow eyes. There were 6 and 7 armed machines hanging from large steel beams, carrying and moving each v-type to the next station.

The carrousel of creation was alive with plastic and silicone, and endless mechanical rearrangement. I felt a sense of pride knowing that I helped create this, I helped build this pyramid, even if I was one of thousands.

When I arrived, I was greeted by a high model v-type, I had never seen one up close. I knew that their body appearance is completely preferential, but I wasn't expecting such a sleek creature.

This v-type was ichorous black, with two gleaming green eyes and four arms, two of which rested motionless on a simple metallic desk. The creature informed me that due to my loyalty to the Church of Loa, I was eligible for a 3rd layer burial at the time of my future demise. My name would be inscribed in the history of the pyramid, remembered by all higher v-type models.

I agreed of course, such an honor to be physically part of monolith. I was given a new designation by the Church. I am now Horus 5.7, in a way I feel reborn as a small piece of flesh supporting a pillar of steel. I know my place is secured among the honored dead.

Doctor Duality's Dialectical Dissertation #7:

I consider myself an amateur in the realm of divinity. I have looked into the black pit of history and read enough holy books to develop a fascination of god and gods. They compel me in some way, some sort of focus draws my attention to their history, particularly that of dead gods.

If you permit me a small description of a few of the dead gods currently orbiting the imagination of a dead dreamer, I will reveal the source of my fascination. The first is that of a fictional deity named Cynothoglys, the great mortician god, the god of rot, the mumbling mouth of the black beyond.

Cynothogyls is symbolized with a single arm, whose hand supposedly embalms all things, so they may decay back into an indistinct void. No one had ever offered sacrifices to Cynothogyls, the idea is purely a recreational one. The idea that all things decay, all things writhe in the ancient rite of transformation. In the transformation of decay and rot, a filament of mold grows in the universe. For those unfamiliar with molds, they can offer an antiseptic quality to their environment, dissolving the variety of other microbial inhabitants. This antibiotic quality ensures their environment is sterile enough for the propagation of its own mechanism.

This idea of a cosmic mold, a high-powered creature that breaks down all things is not unique. A common example is the archetype of the sin-eater, something that decomposes a moral taboo into an object of value, or salvation. The next deity in the spotlight is the goddess Tlazolteotl, she is the South American authority of filth, gold and transmutation. She would convert the very waste of humanity into pure gold. She was culturally adopted by the Aztecs, from the Mayans. She is sometimes depicted in the act of childbirth.

The Mayans threw a bunch of other miscellaneous ideas into Tlazolteotl, from purification to an incidental patroness of adultery, her crown is attributed to a wide variety of human experiences. Not that any of this symbolism did anything for the poor Mayans whose fate is a reminder that civilizations are mortal and decay back into the indistinct void.

From the high tower of historical reflection each god or goddess rises to a crown of importance, and then ebbs like a tide, into the black waters of history. A meta observation of such a mechanism reveals that perhaps the gods themselves are nothing more than by-products of the ad-hoc culture of the time. This kind of reasoning seems fairly common for those looking at the variety of the world, where endless deities are exalted unto altars. The gods seem to be unwilling puppets of the societies which they are birthed from.

There are thousands more of such symbolized deities, each one a decaying god which is no longer part of the human imagination. These dead gods have slowly disintegrated into lost mindscapes, pieces of existential values inherited through circumstantial geography or cultural assimilation. This decaying process is the source of my fascination.

How does one deity rise to cultural importance, then after hundreds or thousands of years decay slowly and is forgotten? Such a question brings me to another deity that perhaps illuminates this question further. The Hindu god Brahma, often depicted as a Holy Cow. The Brahma has a particular form, or conceptualization called Nirguna. In this form, or concept, Brahma is formless, or "without qualities".

The formlessness of Brahma reveals part of my fascination; gods, as they dissolve into history they show a type of high water mark. Over and over; today's Jesus Christ is tomorrow's Glycon, or Marduk. Culture pop icons in a rotating pantheon, passing from one primordial darkness into another.

Perhaps you have heard of human beings referred to as a virus, or bacteria? This observation is meant to be demeaning, as though human beings were microbes in a larger world. I assert that if we are going to be compared in such a way, I think we would be closest to the molds, decomposing cousins in ape shape. We carry on the family tradition of the antiseptic microbes, but rather than biological breakdowns we decompose the annals of history. Each generation forgetting a little more until old stories pass into an unreadable book.

To expand this thought a little; *our* fascination with divinity is the decomposition of our ancestors, a cultural compost bin. Our antiseptic presence scours the pages of history, and the eons pass unremembered.

These ponderings make me second guess my actions when cleaning the green plastic yard waste bin. I spray it out with a hose and scrub it with water. Every year the legions of mold return and I wonder: Am I wiping out microbial religions from the world? Should I let its antiseptic onslaught continue and perhaps work in collusion with such a single-minded creature?

However, I am the larger creature and the scouring of the green plastic bin with the invasive mold is an easy task. Even in victory I reflect on the inevitability of my adversary. If I lax for one season the mycelium will return and their colonies multiply into the decaying filaments.

The Fuse box:

The two men couldn't have hurried any faster, urgency boiled their brains. One carried a small black briefcase and the other fingered a pair of pliers. The briefcase offered no clues to its contents nor did the black leather seem important to the two men. They were primarily occupied with the pliers.

They were bent over a tangle of electronics, wires leading to what may be considered an explosive. The pliers passing back forth between the two men in silence. Slowly the tangle seemed to resemble a more orderly thing, the wires attached to the device in short and understandable distances.

When the two men stepped back from their work the focus of their work became easy to see. They were repairing a fuse box, the briefcase was stored in the basement and obstructed access to the fuse box. The briefcase was then placed carefully against the wall. The two men returned to their sense of urgency as their quest continued through the house.

The basement of the detangled fuse box contained a curious amount of kitchen cabinets. At least 3 distinct sets of cabinetry were piece mealed into the corners of the basement. One of such cabinet sets was quite close to a moist cement wall. Rot had taken hold and been ignored. Each year, the house had slipped deeper into the Kingdom of Dust.

The two men contorted slightly around the cabinet sets, navigating their way to the stairs. Behind them a sharp sound resembling nails across a glass window startled the men. When they turned to the source of the sound, nothing was to be found. The basement had windows that reached exactly ground level, unused, except perhaps for a little sunlight to come into the dark.

If there was something on the other side of the glass basement windows, it did not reveal itself. The men looked cautiously at each other, acknowledging that they heard the sound. The sound repeated again, interrupting the speculation with a sliver of panic. The men were able to catch the source this time. The tiny yellow feet of a chicken could be seen at the edge of the window. Then as the men watched, a small beak raked across the window, repeating the sound again in clear view.

The sense of order eased the tension of the two men, who like most human beings despise the unexplained. As if renewed by the conclusion of the chicken, they hurried up the stairs to see if their fuse box surgery facilitated electricity.

The surgery was a success as the lights in the house became responsive. Licks of light flooded the hallways and lost corners. The house groaned, waking up from a long slumber hurt. The bathroom fans whirled up in noisy complaints, and from another room an old radio screamed out static. The two men rushed to the radio room, quickly silencing the senseless scream from the dead frequency.

The silence returned to the room and the two men nervously looked at each other again with questioning eyes. The radio lay still only for a moment before sparking near the wall, dust and age had created a short. The radio shot back on, this time to a clear frequency. The men watched and listened for a few paralyzing seconds. The smoke growing near the wall, but the surprise held them still.

The song floating from the radio, a version of "I'll Fly Away" and for a measure, the two men listened: "I'll fly away old glory, I'll fly away in the morning, When I die, Hallelujah, by and by, I'll fly away"

When the verse finished, the radio stopped as another electric pop ended the moment. The smoke settled, and the two men returned to their near panicked state. The radio was dead, the power was out again and that would mean another trip into the basement to reset the fuse box.

Their domestic necromancy rested on those lyrics, raising the house back out of the Kingdom of Dust.

Nine Lives:

Thump-thump-thump the wheelbarrow man walked down his stairs to his basement. He had put his tools away already and stood the wheelbarrow up against the shed. Exhaustion had firmly planted his boots in quicksand. He slouched slightly as he reached the bottom stair.

The basement was a concrete cave, illuminated with a single chain switch light bulb. The man stored all his memories in the basement, things that he didn't want to decompose. He kept them tightly sealed away from the wind and sun in a series of cloth bags.

He had collected 14 of such bags, filled with movie ticket stubs, and photographs. He liked paper keepsakes and knew how vulnerable they were to rot. Today was the death-iversary of his parents. It had been 10 years since they died, both falling into the grave within 3 weeks of each other, starting with his father's heart attack.

After the wake he moved back in to take care of his mother, but she was inconsolable. She didn't go to the funeral, she didn't want to talk to her friends or anyone else in the family. She curled up in her bed and her heart fell into pieces. Like glass shattering in slow motion, there was only one outcome. The second funeral was lonely, and the house was left empty.

The wheelbarrow man was tired today, so this trip would be short.

He moved a few bags around and made a path to the back of the basement. At the far end there was a small wooden door, he unlatched it with his elongated fingers, burroughed and knobbed with arthritis. The door creaked open and revealed a small red bag of bones. The wheelbarrow man fingered the bones for a few minutes, carefully looking over their bleached contours.

The bones were feline, an old childhood cat, long since gone to rot. The wheelbarrow man put the bones away, relocked the door and shuffled the bags back into place. With heavy boots he dragged himself back up the stairs and retired into the night.

Down in the basement the bones stirred. The feline legs and ribs, arms and fangs drew themselves together. Its flesh may have been returned to the dirt, but the bones still hissed with life. The bones chattered softly in the dark, its eyeless body squirmed in the red bag. The dead feline dreamed of the deep heartbeat of the earth. The cat could hear the dirt and soil wiggle with worms and beetles, the sound warmed its bones for a moment with the heat of decay.

This night was different, the wheelbarrow man had not been diligent in relocking the little wooden door. The feline bones woke from the dead dream and pushed the door open with its little cat claws. The creek went unheard and the cat started its scratchy crawl over the bags. The dead need no light, they have time. Hours later the small skeleton made it to the base of the stairs leading up. The back legs were malformed, they didn't gather like the front claws, they were twisted and broken, not enough joints or pieces. The half-formed cat started its crawl up the stairs.

The other dreamer in the house was the wheelbarrow man, he was dreaming of nothing. His life had long since decayed, and in a way, was made out of the bones of his memories. The man snored slightly as his breath rattled out of his chest. He did not hear the cat bones pulling themselves up the stairs.

The cat bones got to the top and through instinct checked the location where its food and water dish used to be placed. The bones could not see and could not hear, they were animated by the memories of the wheelbarrow man. The bones only could feel the pull of the strings coming from the bedroom.

The little disfigured bone pile dragged itself down the hall to the bedroom, the snores grower louder.

Once inside the bedroom the cat bones pulled itself unto the bed and curled into a pile at the feet of the wheelbarrow man. The pile pulsed with the snores, matching the beat of deep sleep. With each breath the snores began to slow. Soon the breathing was barely there, and only a soft whisper escaped the man's lips.

He woke briefly to see the pile of bones at his feet, smiling he sat up. He saw a warm black cat at his feet, mewing softly. He gave the warm creature a gentle pet and laid back down. The glamour of his memories faded as his eyes closed. The pile of bones laid still as the last beats of the wheelbarrow man drifted off into the cold deep, the last of his memories decaying into the night.

The Lamp Post:

The heart of nowhere is a place without an entrance or an exit. I dreamt myself there once, there was a lamp post, a soft warm light on a tall post. It was warm and stagnant, no wind blew here, no rain, no clouds, no stars. The lamp post was bright enough that every feature that could have been seen was washed out.

The lamp post radiates light only for so far, then the sky becomes a thick blanket.

I am here, unable to remember how I got to this place. I don't know whether or not I have been here before. Thinking for a brief moment of all the things I have yet to do, things I was concerned with, chores, tasks, alarm clock times that need to be set. Meetings, cleaning, things that are late that need to be tended, apologies to make, people to keep in touch with, ovens to turn off, pets to feed, cars to maintain, it's past the mileage. So many things that I still have to arrange.

In this moment I can't find any way to get back to those things, there is no door or means of transportation. Every moment means one more task disappears, unable to be completed, unable to see the consequence. My poor cat I think, who is waiting for me somewhere far into the opaque greater blackness beyond the lamp post.

As I wait for a time in this soft light oblivion, staring into the bulb of the towering post, each task falls away. Each thing that had to be done will join some decaying world that I can't get back to.

As I wait I grow anxious, no water or food is near, I can only leave this light and venture into the dark. There is only one choice, to stay or leave. Staying means death, means I will fade as my tasks faded, so the darkness becomes a door.

I begin walking, one foot in front of the other, into the dark, as the lamp post disappears behind me into a single dot of light. Hours pass, and I can't tell if my eyes are closed or open, the only sound is the shuffle of my feet, my breath and a soft warmth that seems to hum, inviting me to lie down.

I walked as straight as I could, it's the only order I can bring, a forward momentum. I still can't tell how long I have been walking and a lump is growing in my throat. I begin thinking of the lamp light, how the soft light at least showed me what my hands looked like.

As I am dwelling on the lamp post I come to a sudden and abrupt stop. A wall beats a dull thud on my head and nose, I realize I was looking down. I stumble back, falling onto the ground. I crawl anxiously on all fours, feeling at the wall in the dark. I feel the ground and the wall as the same warm stone, the same warm surface, without descriptive qualities.

I reach as high as I can, I follow to the right for many steps, no change. I dig my fingertips into the edge where the ground and the wall meet. I feel no dirt, no dust, I taste my fingers, without flavor.

I am now faced with another choice, a road of straight feet back to the lamp post or the walk along the wall without clues or promise.

This is the point I wake up, know that I will always be walking there in that unholy city. I am in bed with my sheets and blankets, a warm light falls over the room. I can't tell if my eyes are open or closed anymore.

Malcolm the Blue:

Here lies Malcolm the Blue, holy knight and leader of men.

Malcolm was born from the very soil of this tomb. He was born to the farmers of this land, who's blood runs with the Black Mothers. Even in being born in the cradle of evil magic, Therin's light shined his life. Malcolm's deeds of life are recorded in other texts, filling libraries for scholars. However, Malcolm's trial of the heart was deeper than the stones in the earth.

Malcolm's crossroads was a fever of faith. Before he perished, he dictated to me the first words of Therin. The following was scribed in his final hours by I, his unnamed chronicler:

When Malcolm was young, the old blood of the Black Mothers boiled up inside of him. He was a wretched creature of rage and violence. He fled his homeland in search of freedom of the blinding clouds of anger. He traveled as an unknown wanderer for years, searching the teachings of old gods, seeking a greater power over his inherited affliction.

It was on the cold mountain of Lysander's Pass did he finally lose himself. For days he wandered on the cold winds and icy cliffs. When his strength ebbed, and his food waned, he reached a divine exhaustion. The white sleet blinding his eyes and the soft snow became his bed roll. This is when Malcolm told me that the light of Therin washed over him. It warmed his bones and eased his shoulders.

It was here in the court of the holy goddess Therin that Malcolm saw her face. He looked upon Therin's light in its pristine awe, his weakened heart crumbled before her and he cowed before her presence. In his surrender Therin offered to free him from his seeking and restless struggle with the black winds of his birth. Therin offered him a charge, a duty which to fill the hole in the deepest part of his heart.

The charge she bestowed unto the shoulders of Malcolm was that he must serve his fellow man, he must protect the weak, defend the lowest of the low, the sick and the dying.

As Malcolm told me these things, the light of Therin glowed within him briefly as if the truth shined out from a memory from that mountain top so many years ago. A pause of breath, then with a sudden jolt he sat up. He then told me the cost, Therin brought with her a warning pairing her charge of divine duty.

The warning was spoken in the bright light of Therin and I would lay my life down in the truth of the words that Malcolm spoke. Therin said that the blood of the Black Mothers can never be laid to a true peace. She warned him that his bones must be placed in the earth of his kin, he must join them in the choir of the dead. While she may give him a lifetime of light, she cannot roll back of the tide of his birth.

Malcolm wept at this recounting of memory before his last moments. He told me in his black hour that even with all the powers of light, that darkness comes to us all, to all kingdoms, to all things. Malcolm seemed to grieve a moment, sinking into the knowledge that darkness would eventually come to Therin at some distant time.

When Therin had shined her light upon Malcolm, he woke on that spire of Lysander to a pair of shaking hands. A merchant was travelling the pass in eager risk. Malcolm did not speak much for weeks keeping his burning thoughts to the privacy of his skull.

The merchant was the first to call Malcolm the Blue. For the sight of his bloodless face was a pale blue, and in his bloodlessness, found a moment of freedom from his family's infection.

So here lies Malcolm the Blue, who in his closeness to death, found the light of Therin for the fleeting moments of his life.

Malcolm the blue,

Born with one left shoe,

And a back to work the land,

Therin's light,

Shined in his night,

And turned his heart to hand,

When he fell,

In shine and shimmer,

His blood had turned to sand,

Buried again,

In dank and dark,

Beneath his dead mother's land.

16 Sledgehammers:

The gang of masked figures scurried past the lampposts of a strip mall parking lot. They wore black hoods, they covered their hands, and all wore very similar jackets. On the back of their jackets was a patch resembling a radiant sun, the rays of light replaced with sledgehammers. The number 16 clearly displayed at the bottom. This was their third hit this week and likely the authorities would be closing in soon.

They knew there was a timer, that was part of the plan. Long range observational cameras scanned automatically and looked for pre-programmed images, images like the radiant 16-hammer jacket patch. Today's cameras could see for at least a dozen miles, zoom in on a face or detail with crystal clarity. Higher resolution was possible yet unnecessary due to the thousands of redundant image points. The gang was in Big Brother's house and he was watching.

The 16 shadows said nothing, they crowded around the corner of a strip mall clothing store. They formed two lines of 8 on each side of the corner. The front figures raised their sledgehammers, a 16lb creature of kinetic destruction. They hammered the corner in unison, each taking a few swings, then shuffling to the back of the line, repeating again with the next masked figure.

The hammer strikes sounded like a dull thunder crack, each blow weakening the cement corner. They hammered the corner for 4 minutes, the figures panting from exhaustion. At the end of the 4 minutes the corner crumbled. Then with a silent nod all 16 of the shadows let out a series of rapid strikes against the surrounding cement wall. A greater part of the building corner crumbled. This business would have to be closed for at least a few days for repair, maybe longer.

The enforcement drones arrived 23 seconds late, the gang had fled into the night. The drones scanned the area in spiral formations looking for anything or anyone. There was nothing to be found, except fleeting shadows and empty parking lots. The rumble was a monument to their discipline.

The video finished with the drone feed looking into the night sky after its spiral patrol was finished. The agent scratched his chin slowly, no clues for a cold case. Oliver was hired specifically for this job, under the table, off the books, a last resort kind of job. He liked being off the books and the chance to do some non-public work sounded appealing.

Oliver wasn't overly fond of surveillance, but the money was better than anything he had seen recently. He knew there was a social pressure applied to people when they knew they were being watched, they behaved differently. Usually, if people don't see the drones or the cameras they forget about surveillance. The masked figures in the video feed knew they were being watched, they knew the reaction time of the enforcement drones.

Oliver was a clairvoyant, he could read people in a cold minute. He knew how to manage the most difficult people, the grieving, the confused, the demented and the eager. He mused for a moment, he probably wasn't the only under-the-table agent they had working on this. He started the video feed over again, he was determined to find a clue, something that revealed some personality flaw, some profile detail the inhouse professionals had missed. He reviewed all the older feeds of previous attacks as well. The execution of the other sledgehammer assaults was identical.

Technology allowed Oliver to enjoy 3 more cups of coffee from the comforts of his home while investigating the video feeds. He watched each frame, gave each moment a careful inspection, and pondered as to why such a group would crush the corner of a building. Terrorism was his first guess, but that was lazy, that was an easy answer to plug the hole of senselessness.

He attempted to form a theory: The patches and jackets must have been purchased or produced somewhere. The gang would have to physically meet up somewhere. There was no information from any of the social feeds regarding anything related to: sledgehammers, ire towards the targeted businesses, or the symbolism used in the gang's patches.

Oliver had dead end of cases before, the lack of information, the lack of avenues to search. Maybe he couldn't figure this one out and would have to notch it up to failure and move on. He needed to get his feet on the ground, he needed to go for a walk. The gang might be connected to the businesses near the attacks. He needed more insight, something to jar lose the ice-cold avenues of the case.

He grabbed his winter jacket and a flask of scotch for the walk. Oliver parked his car in the same parking lot that the masked assailants had ran through the night before. He started walking, pretending he had somewhere to go. He watched people from the corners of his eyes, a technique he learned early in life. People behave differently when they are watched, you need to appear invisible, uninterested and most importantly; don't linger.

He walked for 3 hours, up and down the strip mall. He visited beauty shops, furniture stores, banks, restaurants, clothing stores, device service stores, and everything in-between. He took a break and got a bite to eat at a white-collar watering hole. The place was packed with energized success monkeys, each resembling the rest, the same styled shirt, the same confident look in their eyes as they recited whatever corporate mantras they knew.

Oliver watched carefully while he nursed his drink and ate his overpriced meal. There was a shadow here that seemed to grow over the minutes. He had seen the shadow before, like a snake or a serpent, a dim blind spot was coiling around the room. He felt his forehead bead in a cold sweat, something was here, something was watching him.

Oliver's first reaction was to pay his bill and continue his walk, but he needed more information. He wiped the sweat with his napkin and ordered another drink. He did his best to pretend, he was a practiced hand at stoicism. The shadow wasn't visible yet, but the conversations of the clean-cut businessmen started to change. They began stuttering, slurring and muddling their words, yet no one within earshot seemed to notice.

The effervescence of his scotch and soda seemed to hiss, the dialog of the nearby table turned into stammering non-sense: "The d-d-dirt that cannot r-r-rot will live, whe-whe-whether we t-t-turn the w-w-worms or not. "

Oliver's head began to spin, and he felt a high-tension pressure of his brain telling him to run. He left some currency on the table and tried his best to calmly walk out of the restaurant. He looked back when he reached the street. He couldn't see into the windows, there was a kind of darkness cast over the place, he could barely make out the lights or the figures within. The hiss was still ringing in his ears.

He walked home thinking on the experience. Maybe there was something in this town that the drones couldn't see, a greater shadow of a larger predator. The 16 Sledgehammer gang had more to it than simple destruction. He was going to have to go back to the restaurant if he wanted answers, but not tonight, tonight he needed a strong drink and a locked door.

Oliver woke to a sunny day and a headache. The night before had spun him out, the shadow in the restaurant had seen him and revealed something to him. The words still clear in his head, like a bell ringing a panicked alarm: "The dirt that cannot rot will live, whether we turn the worms or not." Who or what were the worms? What dirt? While symbolism was his bread and butter, the language of the occult, he had no real insight.

While he was great at reading people, sizing them up and noticing small details, he was out of his element on this one. He needed something to hide himself from the shadow in the restaurant, he felt in his bones that an answer lay in that sterile strip mall eatery. He poured himself a cup of coffee and carefully thought out a plan.

Later in the afternoon black clouds had rolled in and with it, a little inspiration. His typical method was to research and maybe pay for information. This was different, the shadow was unlikely to be visible to the cameras of the enforcement drones. He knew there were larger creatures out there in the darkness and he had survived so far by steering clear.

His plan was simple: he would shave, buy some new clothes and wear a premeditated story. He would blend in, become just another straight tie with a portfolio. He had nice portfolio himself, so it would be easy to embellish. He would try his best to get on the other side of the shadow, find the relationship with the place and perhaps the gang of the 16 Sledgehammers.

It took a day or two to get the right look; he got his hands manicured, bought a nice suit, purchased some colored eye contacts and an overly expensive pair of shoes. He researched a decent back story, practiced some corporate jargon and nailed the corporate gait.

At the end of the 2nd day there was another Sledgehammer attack in the same area. This time the attack was on a bank, nothing was robbed but one of the walls was reduced to rubble. The news was calling it an act of terrorism. The enforcement agency sent Oliver the video feeds of the drones. There was nothing different about this attack. When the nighttime clouds rolled in, he put on his corporate costume, prepared his lines and walked in the restaurant of the shadow once again.

The crowd was thin tonight, only a handful of after-hour creatures refreshing themselves. He ordered his drink and settled in, he listened and waited for the hiss. The wait wasn't long, an hour into his wait and he saw the shadow. The slithering dark came from behind a window as if the night had poured into the restaurant, the shadow didn't notice him, and Oliver didn't feel the cold sweat this time.

He watched from the corners of his eyes, pretending to small talk up a singleton at the bar, discussing mundane facts about real estate. He saw the dark figure float around the room, landing for a few moments on different people's heads. The host of the shadow would stutter and murmur, then the dark thing would pass onto the next restaurant patron. None of the patrons seemed to notice the nighttime possession, they seemed unperturbed by the change in speech or even aware that anything unusual had happened to them.

Oliver watched the shadow creep around the room, from person to person, head to head. The murmuring words stammered out the same senseless line: "The dirt that cannot rot will live, whether we turn the worms or not." The repetition began to unnerve Oliver and he began seeking the room for the waitress, he thought it may be a good time to steer clear. He found her near the bar taking an order. She turned around and Oliver made eye contact with her. The waitress's eyes were jet black and before Oliver could stand up or turn away the black eyes pinned him down. Shadow poured from the black orbs in her head, Oliver sat transfixed in terror as the shadow weaved itself across the restaurant. The shadow poured itself into Oliver, filling his head with the voluminous mass of darkness. The patrons stopped briefly and looked over at Oliver's motionless body, they all smiled in a delighted unison and then resumed eating their meals and exercising their mouths.

Oliver felt himself screaming, he felt his vocal cords straining and stretching. He couldn't hear anything, he was buried in a sea of thick blackness. Beneath his hands he could feel soil, clumps of earth squeezed tight by his clenched fists. He tried to open his fists, but they began to fuse into his palms, and then his legs and arms felt tightly bound. Oliver squirmed as much as he could, he thrashed and wiggled until he was exhausted. Blind, bound and tired he lay still a few moments.

He could feel himself breathing, his lungs were moving but air wasn't going in, it was the vaporous black. The shadow was inside him, it swayed and rocked him. His squirming turned to writhing and soon his body moved with a graceful and fluid crawl. The dark swallowed him up and he fell beneath the horizon of consciousness.

A few days later there was another sledgehammer attack, this time there were 17 assailants, the patch on their jackets had changed slightly to reflect the increase in membership.

Steel Heart:

The train was a relic, a museum keepsake that could move your bones from one place to another. They don't use trains anymore for mass transit, the infrastructure is too demanding. Now it's all plastic vehicles with onboard monitoring. Trains are *old-fashioned*.

Some of us like the old vibe, the plunge into one's imagination of what it was like to ride the train. I like the idea of the older style mass transit. I heard that some people used trains for business commuting, everyday riding, dawn-treading, midnight meetings in train car 3 with endless bourbon. I wanted a piece of that, just a little taste. I paid good money to ride this relic.

The train was clean, yet a little ragged. The tour conductor made mention several times that the seats were clean, despite their used posture. We were shown where the tickets would be displayed, they showed the size the bathrooms, the mechanism for opening and closing doors. The doors had all been refitted with automatic openers, cameras and photo locations peppered the train cars. You could get one of the countless photos that were taken periodically printed out on physical paper and framed as a memento if you desired.

Some of the insincere tourism disenchanted me, but after an hour looking outside and a couple Bloody Marys, I was getting into the experience. I opened my device and read the history of train routes, pausing now and again to gaze out at the beautiful water. The route of this train was cresting the edge of a calm and peaceful tide. The water was glass, the train ride was pleasant and the chatter of folks in my train car put me into a sleepy stupor.

I dreamt of the train engine, the hot metal beat of a steel heart. The bright gleam of the used rails, the worn wheels spinning with their angled arms attached in a repetitive march. It was building up, a powerhouse rushing down a thin line, predetermined. The engine felt utterly single minded, something I haven't felt in a long time. I was enjoying the dreamscape, then the course turned, racing around a bend. I saw a freeway overpass with the graffiti "Labrat" sprayed on the concrete bridge. I felt a sinking feeling as the train derailed, that explosive single mindedness recklessly shook me awake.

I looked around quickly, taking a quick inventory of myself. It was just a dream, I was still in the train car travelling at a peaceful speed around the edge of the glassy water. The emergency stayed with me though, I could feel the engine still, the steel heart thumping. While half in my dream hangover and the other half ordering another drink, I found myself moving closer to the front of the train. I wanted to hear the engine beat louder.

When I got to the front car it was crowded. We were shoulder to shoulder, everyone had given up on comfortable personal space. I nudged my way up to the front, everyone looked a little spaced out. Their eyes were glossed over and staring at the door to the engine room. I could feel the reason why; the engine was quite pleasant to listen to. The "chugga chugga" turned over from the iron and steel, oil and leverage. I felt that reason grow a little bit louder. Then it hit me, I could feel the beat, the rhythm of the engine. Such an experience was new to me, I had not expected this. Something like this was more primitive than train details and sweeping landscapes. This was an entirely unexpected immersion.

As these thoughts, a self-awareness washed over me, I found myself standing and staring with the same glossy eyes as these strangers. I closed them and could see it clearly: An iron and steel machine, molten veins pumping the blood of an ancient technology, like the heart of an angry beast. The weight of its rhythm pouring me into it, the hot fires of frequency, the rail bound destination that was unalterable. The single line of purpose was intoxicating.

The frontmost train car was very warm with all those people, all that internal combustion. I got lost in it for a few minutes and then shuffled out. I passed by people moving in and could see the same yearning in their faces, right about to surface. I was satisfied for now, I returned to my seat, and soon the train came to the end of the trip. I bought a couple pictures in the gift shop and decided to schedule another trip for the following year. I thought to myself that this would be a great tradition, to return to the great steel beating heart. Perhaps a part of me is a bit *old fashioned*.

The Tide:

The Black Ship docked yet again in a shallow port. The masts and deck left empty, no people to be seen pulling any ropes or guiding the rudder to the dock. The ship was tied to the moorings with an oily black rope. The waves scraped the tar and wood hull against the cement sides. The ship looked out of time, surrounded by cargo ships, full to the tops with containers. The small black ship offered no explanations, no clues could be seen upon initial inspection.

The harbor master and a few workers boarded the ship in cautionary investigation. The hull was empty, not a single provision or object was discovered. No bodies or trash or rot, not a single sign or clue. The workers and harbor master scratched their heads and questioned each other on possibilities. Some thought to ask the dock workers that were on shift last night, perhaps check the security cameras to see if anyone had left or entered the dock. The ship certainly didn't tie itself to the dock, someone must know who it belonged to.

The records were checked and the cameras reviewed. They questioned the other workers, looking for anything that might be out of place. Nothing was found and the head scratching continued. By the second day the harbor master was contacting their superiors for advice.

The ship continued to sit in the harbor, the black wood and oily ropes remaining untouched and unused.

On the third day 6 people called in sick. 15 people called in sick by the 4th day. There was nothing on the news until the 5th day. By then it was too late.

Day after day people stopped coming to work, the roads became empty or sparse. People stopped showing up to grocery stores, in fact they stopped showing up altogether. Their cars remained unused in their driveways or parking lots.

The news station tried to report on the disappearances, there were only a handful of reporters that tried anything. They had no answers either, they speculated a virus or pandemic but no bodies were found. The reporters also scratched their heads in confusion, no clues or answers were given.

Some people tried recording themselves on live feeds in case they disappeared. Those that tried this method found that their viewership disappeared slowly, day after day until no one was watching their live feed. It wouldn't take long and they too would turn their recording off and never turn it back on.

This pattern of investigation continued in every corner of humanity for a few weeks. Each section of human beings dissolving into a quiet disappearance that no one seemed to remember or know anything about.

There were a few live news feeds with people indulging in a few last minute hedonistic fantasies. No police around or anyone to stop them. They broadcasted their feeds in hopes someone else was watching. There were no more watchers.

One of the few remaining was the harbor master. He kept coming to work, regardless of the lack of anything to do. There were no containers to move, no dock workers to manage. No new ships came and nothing needed to be done. The black ship sat untouched by change, floating peacefully out the harbor masters tower window. The black masts slowly bobbing up and down on the horizon as the harbor master sat wondering what to do.

Work had been the only focus that survived in the face of the meaningless disappearance. He had ritualistically gone to work at the same place for the last 25 years and it was the only thing that kept him from grabbing his head and screaming his brains out. Now the only thing to do was sit and wait, wait for whatever had claimed everyone else, to now claim him. If he waited then surely, he would get some sort of answer.

The answer didn't come, and day after day he grew numb staring out the window of the harbor master tower. The black ship bobbed up and down, seemingly the only thing that moved on the horizon. The large container ships were far too large for harbor waves to animate at all. The black ship was a lure, a worm on a hook. It was waiting for him to walk aboard it, at least that is what the harbor master's brain started to tell him.

Day after day this idea seemed to grow, it swelled up like a late morning headache. It started to replace any other ideas in the harbor master's head. There wasn't anything else going on anyways, there were no other people, nothing else to do and nowhere to go. This was the only show in town and the black ship was quite distinguished next to the giant container ships. The ichorous creature occupied his daily thoughts as his daily ritual fell apart.

On a beautiful Sunday afternoon, he packed his bags, as if he was going on a vacation. He boarded the black ship with a suitcase. He sat down on the deck and waited. He was used to waiting, he had spent the greater part of the past few weeks waiting to disappear like everyone else. Nothing happened at first, he sat and waited and finally fell asleep.

In his sleep he dreamt of bright hued music that fell over the sky in sunset colors. A choir rose up in his slumber and trumpets blared out a triumph. The music washed over the black ship like a storm, the noise of orange and blue, purple waves and pink clouds of turbulent winds. The whole of the sky was alive in a fantastic motion, a nausea of whirling voices.

The harbor master awoke to a wide ocean. No land was seen in any direction. He watched the endless horizon day after day without a single change. Each night the same dream entered him. Food and water did not seem to be needed, no hunger or thirst. The days turned to a static of unchanging waves and the night alive with swirling colors and choirs.

It would be weeks of this night and day, each day felt shorter and each night longer. Eventually there was no more daytime and he disappeared completely into his dreams, he was gone, dissolved from the unchanging ship and empty horizon.

Claws:

Monday morning was just like any other Monday, the world was spinning in a meaningless circle of terrifying possibilities. Technology propped up a couple trillion human beings, all which wanted dignity. Power games played out in predictable irattational ways, governments were in the process of decay and decomposition. Giant corporations finally removed the last barrier of limitation and had installed their own armies.

People of all types clung to their tribes, finding ways to warm themselves regardless of the swirling world around them. One such tribe is a life advocacy group. They call themselves New Life, a moral group. New Life advocates of all life, plants and animals, even microbes. They consider antibiotics and vaccines to be genocidal. Their views are considered extreme by most. In certain corporate territories their views are illegal and anyone associating with New Life members may find themselves removed from their corporate insulation of comfort and ease.

New Life membership has decreased in the past years, people writing the movement off as a fad, a flash in the pan silliness. Their numbers however have been hidden, obscured by a cult-like behavior. Finding ways of communication outside of the electric eye of technology. This particular Monday morning, the mostly ignored New Life cult is about to receive a new initiate.

Bethany Ultrix woke up on a beautiful sunny day. She felt deeply connected to the world around her, as if she could reach out and touch the faces and names of her dreams. Last night's slumber had been unusually vivid, one of the faces looked like an old woman, but without lips, as though her mouth was no longer needed. The mouth looked slack, but Bethany could hear words coming from her, little messages from inside her head.

Bethany showered and started to get ready for her day. She stopped suddenly in front of the mirror, examining a small 4-lined scratch on her leg. The thin cuts didn't hurt, she probably wouldn't have noticed them if her reflection didn't tell her. She shrugged as something inside told her not to worry about it. The same something inside told her not to go to work and to skip breakfast. She wasn't hungry, and work would understand. She still made coffee out of habit.

She sat in her front room with her coffee, staring out the window. She spaced out for a couple hours and her coffee cooled in an unused stillness, the cream forming tiny white rivers. She regained focus slowly in the afternoon and decided to make a Reflection entry. There was a small panic inside her, something was wrong, but another tide swallowed the panic up and eased her back into the comfortable chair.

Bethany Ultrix #Reflection Hour: 15:48:

I feel so small today. The door seems so big, my chair seems so wide and it takes me forever to cross the room. I keep having these ideas today; I need to walk somewhere but I don't know the address, there is something important to learn, some piece of information that will explain this smallness.

I looked outside today and felt like I wasn't a human being anymore, my body feels no larger than a chair cushion. The window looked like a towering gate of light, the sun burning overhead so slowly I could see the pale beams. The dust motes were floating in the air, like an ocean of creatures swimming down to the bottom of a sea of sunlight.

**End Reflection Hour

Bethany put down her device and held her head in pain. A clear image interrupted the pleasant recollection of the mindless morning. The image was a path drawn in unwavering light. She could see each step to the location, each street name, each turn of the road. When the pain passed, she grabbed her coat and shoes and hurried out the door. She knew where the face with the lipless slacked mouth of her dreams was, the location was clear and simple.

She walked with a determined pace, each moment seemed to bring a sense of comfort, as if forgotten questions were about to have answers. Who she was, what her life meant, where her place in the universe was, it all seemed as though it was rising to the surface within herself. She thought clearly while traveling to the vivid location in her mind, the directions proving accurate.

The closer she got to the destination the clearer the questions became. The answers seemed to fall out of her head in perfect response: Who am I? "You aren't anything, everything you do, all your preferences, habits, genetics, they all connect to others, your self-identity will bleed away into your actions. There is no separation, we aren't anything." The monolithic absence of a dissolved self was comforting, the question settled and became silent.

Closer and closer she came to the destination and the questions rose like an alarm, and the answers muffled them: What is my purpose, where is my place in the universe? "The only purpose of life is to continue life. Any other purpose is the denial of life." The clarity rung true for Bethany, who by this time was having a hard time remembering that she was called Bethany. She couldn't find a flaw in the logic, her brain felt like it was moving in slow motion and accepted the internal dialog as her own.

Within the biological mechanism of Bethany Ultrix there was a new organism growing. A tiny colony of bacteria, this bacterium had learned that human beings were amazing vehicles for its procreation, they were like comets or space ships, able to traverse massive distances to spread its own microbial genetic information. For the bacteria, Bethany had walked for a duration of 14 generations of binary fission, plenty of time for the bacterium to develop answers to Bethany's questions of existential doubt.

Bethany arrived at the decaying house in the late evening. The windows were open, and the door left unlocked. The roof sagged with rot and the gutters overflowed with slime. She entered the house silently, knowing she would find the slack-mouthed woman of her dreams here. She had no doubts.

The old woman sat on a small metal chair, her eyes darting around the room as her body remained motionless. Bethany drew close to the lady and gently touched her hand. As she did, the thoughts of the old woman pierced her brain, the thoughts rung like heavy bells. The sound cleared the last sense of identity that she had, it wiped her memories, her ego, everything down to basic instincts. Bethany dissolved away by the weight of the bell ringing.

The colony of bacteria now held all the strings of Bethany's brain. The rotten-house woman had done her job, the lipless mouth had said nothing.

The next day Bethany woke up on the floor of the rotten house. Her eyes glassy and empty. Over the night and from the tips of her fingers grew sharp talons. They had grown 2 inches and were quite thin, nearly the width of a kitten's claw.

Bethany, who was not Bethany any longer, was filled with a singular urge, a divine spark of purpose. The thunderstorm within her head rolled through her brain and Bethany ran out the door. Within 20 minutes she found a human being in their garden, bent over and weeding.

She snuck up behind them and with an effortless swipe she clawed the back thighs of the oblivious gardener. The claws delivered a colony of bacteria. The thin scratches were marked in divine purpose. Bethany who was not Bethany smiled in satisfaction. The gardener reeled around to see a woman running off down the street.

The Sermon of the Iron Caldron:

The room smells like sandalwood, someone has prepared the mood. The candlelight roams the walls in flickering shadows. The floor is grouted in smooth tiles and stained in a red ichor. At its center sits a large iron caldron.

There are only ghosts that use the room these days, wispy leftovers preserved in ritual. Some human beings keep the candles refreshed and the air sweet, but they are only caretakers, decorated janitors for a place abandoned of its original purpose.

The frail ghosts will not speak, nor use their useless spectral limbs for anything other than mimicking the shadows. Their memories have all but dissolved into the salty brine of time. Yet a few remain, a few still sing their songs of the dead. Their afterlife vocal organs producing vague sounds resembling wind blowing over the gravestones of forgotten generations. Each song containing a chorus of tattered and disembodied minds. Their ebbing memories forming a single frustrated sound that seems to dwell solely in the hollow chasm of the Iron Caldron at the center of the room.

If the spectral prisoners of the Iron Caldron could speak with human voices and human tongues they would only be able to recite the experience of their imprisonment. Every other aspect of their lives has been burned away.

You would have to turn back the pages of time to the year 350 B.C.E. The great book of human history would illuminate the words from its tattered pages, the contents of spectral imprisonment. Before we read such contents aloud, let us offer the blank pages of history our veins, that one day, we may haunt the living with the dead songs of our deeds.

The great book creaks and whines with the contortion of its spine. Let's focus on the past, let it coalesce and brighten the colors of the shadowed room. Let us read aloud the pages of history:

The Book: Chapter 45742122 Verse 22:

The Iron Caldron has just been installed at the center of the ritual space. Beneath the Caldron are 3 stout pillars with chiseled symbols of dead gods. Busy workers finish the stonework with professional satisfaction. The censers are placed at the edges of the room, they have not yet burned any frankincense or sandalwood, but the supplicants are eager and ready.

We watch as the motion of history whirls by and the room is emptied of the last of the construction. A week passes in silence and no one enters. Then, a new moon rises overhead without a single sliver of white. The night is the deepest black of the year. Robed humans begin a slow and intentional procession into the room. One by one they encircle the Iron Caldron, geometrically spaced, heads bowed in reverent focus.

At the end of a few somber moments each participant produces a leather wineskin and pours the contents into the Iron Caldron. The liquid is a thick syrup of blood, obtained through murder or chance. The blood is that of their enemies; captured marauders, oath breakers and political rivals. Each robed figure pours the blood of this year's enemies into the Iron Caldron.

Kindling beneath the Caldron is added. The fire is lit, and the flame encouraged. Each of the participants watches as the blood boils into a reduction of hard film at the bottom of the Iron Caldron. The fire is left to finish the ritual as the iron of the blood is added to the Caldron's metal body. The participants return to their lives, confident that their enemies are forever imprisoned within the belly of the Iron Caldron.

We can watch this scene from the pages of history, and each year more blood will be poured into the Iron Caldron. We can flip each page and see the same rite, another year of burning the blood. When we have had our fill, our curiosity slaked, we can close the book of history. The spine cracks again as we flip to the blank and pristine pages of the present.

The pages call to us to continue the ritual, to fill the empty pages with our blood and burn the offering. Whether it be in the belly of the Iron Caldron or the actions of our lives, we will all end up on the pages of history.

Armor of the Red Flower:

Albert liked his new vase, a thoughtful gift from a dear friend. The vase was a black and red piece of pottery, well balanced in form and the weight felt stable. The red detail had a pleasant Ikebana stylization to it. Little red swirls resembling flowers climbed up the lips of the opening. Near the bottom, patterns of widely spaced rings descended into tighter lines. The bottom was a deep red ring that illuminated the lighter accents of the top.

Albert had admired the vase for years. He kept it in his front room and often found himself staring into the red rings and swirls of delicate decoration. However, it only takes a reckless moment to shatter such beauty.

The vase was broken with the accidental swing of Albert's travel luggage. This of course happened on his way out the door, rushed and frantic he left the broken pieces to lay in the dark until he returned from his trip. They laid like little bleeding triangle shards. A singular large piece began humming softly a few moments after Albert left to his trip.

The humming grew louder, and although no one was there to witness the growing phenomena, it crackled with an audible rumble and snap. The rumbling focused slightly, and the sounds of metal and leather could be identified. The source of the sound was that of a dark spot that grew at the base of the broken vase. The scene unfolded within a miniature world, were a miniature sun eclipsed the broken pieces of pottery and the floor turned an opaque black.

A few moments later the sound stopped, and the shadow dispersed. The floor was now occupied by a full suit of metallic ebony armor, the shine and gloss reflected even in the late hours of the front room. Day after day the armor sat motionless until Albert returned from his trip. Albert was not expecting to nearly trip over a suit of armor in his front room.

After putting his belongings in their appropriate places and starting his laundry, he investigated what appeared to be a foreign object left by some unknown source. Albert scratched his cheek trying to recall which of his friends would have meant this as a gift, or perhaps a joke which may have sprouted from a drunken conversation in a thrift store. Such occurrences were not uncommon for Albert and his friends.

The suit of armor was gathered up and laid on the dinner table. Albert contacted some of his friends and received no clues. He investigated the armor carefully looking for any insight as to who or how this metal and leather thing got into his house. The armor had no tag, no contact information, no contemporary marks of note.

The armor was composed of a black metallic breast plate in the style of a conquistador, like two clam shells coming together in the center of the chest. Leather straps lined the shoulders and sides. There seemed worn and used. The vambraces and pauldrons were shelled slightly, layered pieces of a hammered dull iron composite. Perhaps stainless steel? No rust was discovered or any marks of age other than the worn straps. There was a red lined decoration, very similar to the broken vase.

The red lining resembled flowers, but only on parts of the armor as if the armor was unfinished. The thin flowers were the most detailed on the front of the helmet, which resembled an exaggerated lizard or dragon head. The red lines pouring out of the face plate in rosy swirls.

Without a doubt, the armor fascinated Albert, his brain turning over the mystery, the style, the similar beauty to his broken vase. All the unknowns fogged over his brain as he turned over the pieces and investigated each one precisely. When he looked over the greaves, whose coloring mirrored the base of the vase precisely in deep red lines, he had a most electric idea; the armor would probably fit him.

Albert changed his clothes to fit inside the armor, nothing too heavy or slack. He began at the bottom, strapping the greaves and thigh pieces slowly. Then after seeing them on, his pace quickened. The armor fit exactly, it felt snug and safe, as if the curves and length had been tailored for him. The holes for the straps fell effortlessly into a familiar position. Albert admired himself in the mirror and took a few pictures on his device.

The last piece was the helmet. The chin strap was snug, the inner helmet was comfortable, and again seemed to be made precisely for Albert's head.

Albert looked himself over in the mirror, a black and red warrior. Certainly, someone had determined his measurements and gifted this to him. This wonderful sense of admiration was replaced quite quickly by vertigo. The mirror appeared to be growing larger.

The room stretched out and swelled, the table rose, the windows came alive and reached out to match the dimensions of the front room. The seconds ticked by in a slow-motion panic. The room was growing, he was shrinking, and the armor shrunk with him. He screamed, but only a little squeak escaped the helmet.

Albert frantically tried to remove the armor, however he discovered that his arms and fingers were slowly turning into pottery. His fingers stiffened, and his mouth felt tight. His legs stopped moving and straightened up. He tried to raise his hands to get at the chin strap, but they cemented into place above his head.

As Albert grew smaller, his armor and his body began to fuse together, and within minutes his body could not move at all.

A few hours later, one of Albert's friends came to his house. They could not find Albert, nor the armor he had asked about. They did however find a black and red vase, not in pieces, but fully formed on the floor in front of the mirror. The friend examined the vase and some of the red paint looked fresh, as if a new flower had just been painted on it.

The Rope:

Maria enjoyed her walk home to and from community college. She lived nearby, a small house with her folks. She had graduated high school a year ago, and she was ready to put that chapter of her life in a box somewhere and forget about it. Last year her friend

Fernando had hung himself, 2 days before graduation, the light at the end of the 4-year tunnel had turned into a blinding spotlight.

She wondered if Fernando would have enjoyed community college, he had always enjoyed school, it was the pressure that got him. The suffocation of potential, nailed into his head with hammers oddly shaped like advice. He was dead now and the day was beautiful, the sun flowed down in golden warmth. The trees rustled only a little and fresh smell of the spring quarter had captured Maria's attention.

There were new people and the new world opened up. High school was time served, and now the bright possibilities showed a larger world. The wider vision started the first day at the campus, Maria's imagination blossomed at the vast variety of people, ideas, and topics. High school has a way of shielding children from reality, but here, the world was filled with all sorts of cogs you could be, all sorts of jobs and people you could turn into. Maria had no idea what she wanted to be, but she loved the imagination without the commitment.

Maria's walk to campus went by a freeway on-ramp, a bustle of thousands of cars zooming through the arteries of the city. She thought of cities as living things, with hearts and stomachs and blood vessels, each represented by some function: garbage trucks, fire stations, hospitals, schools and of course skyscrapers. Fire stations reminded her of the human immune system, schools and shopping centers like a stomach filled with nutrients for the social cells to deliver to their ridged cells called houses. Skyscrapers were like mold that developed long and elegant filaments of growth, all around her she saw life, blooming in a symbolic reflection of green fields.

This idea was something she and Fernando talked about at length, her first long conversation. Maria's parents didn't like symbolism or anything with more than one meaning, to them words meant one thing and the city was certainly not anything like the green fields. Those conversations were cut short and diverted towards practical matters like what Maria was going to college for. What job do you want? What are you going to do with your life?

There seemed to be no greater difficulty than trying to determine what she wanted. She wished Fernando was around, sometimes speaking the words was enough, a release of the swirling potential, distilled into plain words. There was nothing quite like getting drunk from the possibilities of youth, swimming into the deep black of the future. The words were not enough for Fernando. The memory soured the walk a little. It had been a year and the pain had ebbed, Maria felt guilty about it, she had vowed never to forget Fernando. After only a year she could feel the memory getting dusty, she winced and continued her walk to campus.

As she passed the freeway on-ramp she noticed a long rope hanging from a street light. The metal pole faced the freeway and the rope dangled just barely above her fingers. Maria felt compelled, perhaps by curiosity, perhaps the strangeness of its placement begging for some sort of conformation of its existence. Maria jumped feebly and grazed the bottom of the rope with her fingers.

Maria put her bags down and positioned herself along side the freeway ramp. She eyed the rope and positioned herself for a better jump. The rhythmic sounds of cars and trucks marched beside her in hazy focus. She jumped and caught the rope with one hand, slipping back to the ground. Redoubling her efforts, she tried again and grabbed the bottom of the rope firmly with both hands, hanging a couple inches from the ground. Maria bent her legs and looked down imagining that she was higher up looking down over a great distance.

The rope was sturdy, and Maria rocked back and forth slowly, like she would as a kid, each pass getting longer and longer. The rope was nearly 30 feet and the rocking covered the ground, not the freeway. She felt a little exhilaration swinging so close to the freeway and started to lengthen the swing. Within a few moments she was traveling the edge of the freeway in pleasant swoops with the feeling of inertia carrying her further each time.

The rope swing was cresting, reaching nearly 180 degrees. Each swing was taking a solid 4 seconds of rushing force, the air turning to wind as her hair blinded her on the return swing. Like on the swing sets of her childhood the swing reached the point of tipping over the top, a huge 30 ft circle trying to complete itself. Her stomach caught up to her throat and she let it out in a scream.

The crest was reached with a momentary lapse of inertia as the force failed to swing over the top. A moment of weightlessness and then a 30-foot plummet down towards the ground. Maria twisted herself and angled her body towards the freeway to try and eat some slack on the rope. Cars and trucks honked helplessly as she plummeted down the first 10 feet, her angle attempt paid off and the twist caused the rope swing to gather some inertia back, swinging her out over the freeway. The motion resembling a tether ball wrapping around a pole.

Maria held on tightly and when the ground was within reach she let go, tumbling onto the grass next to the freeway, her hair echoing the frantic landing. She screamed a small shriek and stopped moving. Her heartbeat pounding out an emergency, her arms exhausted from holding on and her hair wrapping around her face. Maria cleared the hair from her vision and looked at the dangling rope, still alive from the swoop and the swing.

With a smile she gathered her bags and walked the rest of the way to community college. She thought of Fernando again; perhaps there isn't any difference between swinging and hanging.

The End.

Additional stories: Serpentspeaks.blogspot.com

All artwork and edits by Delia Wang

All stories by Raymond Street/Archmonoth 2018

Email: Serpentandcrow@gmail.com

IG/FB: Archmonoth

tombs

& & & & & & & & & & & & & & & &

TOWERS

Made in the USA
Columbia, SC
03 July 2022

62747159R00035